Bringing Braille into the Computer Age

Carrying on the Torch

Robert J. Richey

authorHOUSE®

AuthorHouse™
1663 Liberty Drive
Bloomington, IN 47403
www.authorhouse.com
Phone: 1-800-839-8640

Published by AuthorHouse   5/21/2012

ISBN: 978-1-4685-8475-2 (sc)
ISBN: 978-1-4685-8474-5 (e)

Library of Congress Control Number: 2012906960

Contents

Other Books by this Author

1. Take Time to Smell the Roses Book of Poetry
   a. ISBN # 1-4033-4472-8 (Paperback)
   b. ISBN # 1-4033-8753-2 (Hardcover)
2. The Golden Knight Book of Chess: The Art of Sacrifice
   a. ISBN # 1-4208-6573-0 (Paperback: Text in Black & White)
3. Life on the Diamond Bar Ranch: A Tale of the West
   a. ISBN # 978-1-4259-6451-1 (Paperback 6" x 9")
4. Robinhood of the Underworld: Dominic Capizzi
   a. ISBN # 978-1-4343-1949-4 (Paperback)
5. Life on the Diamond Bar Ranch: A Tale of the West

Foreword

In the year 1809 a boy was born in a small village near Paris. At the age of 3 this boy suffered an accident that resulted in complete blindness. This boy's name was Louis Braille. In a strange way this tragedy led directly to the creation of the Braille Code. This Code for almost 200 years has benefited a countless number of individuals all over the world, who have suffered sight impairment.

In another rather strange way, the writing of this book was also the result of an unusual event.

I have been friends, for many years, with another man who has lost most of his sight. For quite a few of those years, I have taken the friend out to dinner once a week.

One day, several months ago, I dropped the friend off at his home. As I started to leave and head for home, suddenly out of nowhere, I felt a need to visit a Center for the Blind which was located near where I lived. Such a feeling had never happened to me before.

I arrived at the Center for the Blind and entered the front office. When I inquired of the receptionist about learning about the Center, I was directed to the rear of the building. Two very kind older women, who were volunteers, showed me around the room where all of their work was performed. They showed me all of the equipment and explained how it all worked.

Although, I found it fascinating how books and documents were transcribed in Braille, I was almost shocked that the method was so primitive.

I was presented with a brochure containing information about the Braille Code. In this brochure there was a picture of a Biology Text Book, and along with it were 43 volumes that had turned it (the Biology book) into Braille.

These 43 books in Braille were sent out to enable nine (9) blind students to read along with sighted students in a science class. This same office was preparing three more orders each consisting of the same 43 books in Braille.

The preparation of these 43 volumes alone consisted of 3601 pages. When the Order was received by this particular office, thermoform copies of each page had to be made. After the pages of each volume had been made, they had to be punched, bound and labeled.

Thermoform Copying is ingenious, but labor intensive and painfully slow. Each page (in Braille) that is submitted is used as a Master Copy. It is put in a machine and placed under a plastic sheet. The lid of the machine is closed. Heat and pressure are applied to soften the plastic overlay, which settles down around the many dots of Braille. The Master Copy and the plastic copy are removed, and as the plastic copy cools it hardens. This slow process must be performed 3601 times to reproduce all of the volumes.

This Project occupied the volunteers from January 6, 2003 until February 26, 2003. It required a total of 552 hours to complete the job. This number of hours did not include the work the transcribers performed at home on their own computers. Typically it required 30 days for one transcriber to complete just one volume of the 43 books that were needed to complete the total job.

At the present time there are machines that allow individuals to read Braille faster, but they are cumbersome and expensive.

The more I learned about the history of Braille, the more convinced I became that there must be a better way to provide books in Braille for the sight impaired.

Acknowledgement

The Photo on the Front Cover is that of a long time friend; Al Salice. He has visual impairment. It is our friendship that led to the writing of this book.

The Story of Louis Braille

There was a time, not long ago, when most people thought blind people could never learn to read. People thought the only way to read was to look at words with ones own eyes.

A young French boy by the name of Louis Braille thought otherwise. Blind from the age of three, young Louis desperately wanted to read. He realized the vast world of thoughts and ideas were locked out to him because of his disability. He was determined to find a way for a blind people to read.

This story begins in the early part of the nineteenth century. In a village near Paris Louis' father made harnesses and other leather goods to sell to the other villagers. His father often used sharp tools to cut and punch holes in the leather.

One of the tools he used to makes holes was a sharp awl. An awl is a tool that looks like a short pointed stick, with a round, wooden handle. While playing with one of his father's awls, Louis' hand slipped and he accidentally poked one of his eyes. At first the injury didn't seem serious, but then the wound became infected. A few days later young Louis lost sight in both eyes. The first few days after becoming blind were very difficult for him.

As the days went by he learned to adapt to his blindness and to lead an otherwise normal life. He went to school with all his friends and did well in his studies. He was both intelligent and creative. He wasn't going to let his disability discourage him.

According to individuals, who are knowledgeable about such things, a child who loses their sight at that young age does not retain any memory of precise visual images

When he was only nine years old, his father contacted the Minister of the Interior. He inquired if it would it be beneficial for a young child to attend the Institution Royales des Jeunes, Aveugles, which was located in Paris. This school was for the blind.

After a lengthy consideration of the situation, Louis was awarded a Scholarship and was accepted at the school.

It is reported that he began applying himself in all of his studies and soon became an accomplished student. Much later in life, he became a Professor at the same school.

Louis' Arrival at the School for the Blind

When he first arrived at the school for the blind, he asked if the school had books for blind people to read. Louis found that the school did have such books.

However, there was a drawback. These books had large letters that were raised up off the page. Since the letters were so big, the books themselves were large and bulky. More importantly, the books were expensive to buy. The school had only fourteen of them.

He read all of these books in the school library.

He could feel each letter, but it took him a long time to read a sentence. It took a few seconds to read each word, and by the time he reached the end of a sentence, he had almost forgotten what the beginning of the sentence was about. He came to believe that there must be a better way.

There must be a better way for a blind person to feel the words on a page, and to read as quickly and as easily as a sighted person.

That very day he set a goal for himself to think up a system which would help blind people read. He would try to think of an alphabetic code to make his 'finger reading' as quick and easy as sighted reading. As a tremendously creative person, he had learned how to play the cello and the organ at a young age. In fact, he became so accomplished as an organist, that he played at churches all over Paris. Music was really his first love. It also happened to be a steady source of income. He had great confidence in his own creative abilities.

His confidence in himself, and his musical talent, demonstrated how much he could accomplish when given a chance.

The Current Braille System

For over two hundred years the Current Braille System has enriched the lives of countless individuals around the World. Up until this method of being able to "read" the written word; individuals with severe Sight Impairment were limited to verbal communication.

This type of disability has always existed. This inability to communicate with others has prevented them from being fully engaged. But over a span of 200,000 years, it is believed no one has tried to invent a system that would allow blind persons to read.

This change came to pass in the early 1800's. It was brought about by the occurrence of four completely unrelated events. Fortunately, these four events occurred within a short period of time of each other. If any one of them had happened too many years ago, or too many years in the future; the situation would not have changed. These events also happened in the same area. It was vital that all of these events occurred jointly to bring about this historic change.

The French Revolution

The First Event in the chain that led to the Braille Code was rooted in the French Revolution.

In the latter part of the 1700's, there was a restive period in France where large numbers of ordinary people started questioning the way the world order existed.

This occurred in the American Colonies in 1775 when the new Colonists were trying to free themselves from the Yoke the English King was trying to impose on them.

In Europe, and especially in France, new ideas were beginning to cause large numbers of Frenchmen to question everything.

Kings traditionally had the power of life or death over any citizen under their control. Unfortunately, individuals who became King were not always honorable decent human beings. In fact in some places, even a mad man could become King.

Traditionally the Ruler was always from one family. To aid in keeping the peasants under control these individuals had the temerity of declaring that they had the Divine Rights of Kings, implying that the Creator had picked them to lead. Such Gaul!

The period being considered here was between the years 1789-1799. Up until that time the Catholic Church was very powerful in France, as well as elsewhere. The Church did not pay any taxes, but demanded a 10% tithe from its parishioners. Due to this big advantage the Church owned at least 10% of all of Frances' land.

In some countries being a member of the Church (determined by the Monarchy) was mandatory. Heretics were dealt with very harshly. The Inquisition is an extreme example.

Individuals began to preach a different religion where man could pray directly to God without using a church person as intermediary.

To compound the problem the rich became

richer while the poor became poorer. There seemed to be a complete disconnect between the two groups. This sort of situation, if not corrected in a positive way, can lead to a real catastrophe. This is what happened.

This book is not intended to be a history book about France, nor is this writer qualified to write one. This period in French history is mentioned merely to list the underlying forces that led France into war with its neighbors; with starvation among its poorer members and eventually to the Guillotine.

Over time things went from bad to worse. Finally, armed Frenchmen attacked the establishment. One of their targets was a prison named the Bastille. There are those who believe they did this to free political prisoners. However, other sources believe that their target was to bring a large cache of weapons into their possession.

Finally, the French King (Louis XVI) was executed and France became a Republic, although it became a very restive; perhaps unruly Republic.

The Rise of Napoleon Bonaparte as Emperor

Napoleon Bonaparte's rise to power brought an end to the turmoil that had plagued France for so long. A Strong Man had become the Leader of France.

He had been in the French Military and had been a political leader during the latter stages of the French Revolution. His rule as Emperor of France and later King of Italy spanned the years 1804 to 1815.

His introduction of the Napoleonic Code in the field of Law had a major influence on Civil Law all over the world. Also it was instrumental in establishing the Metric System. It is for the Napoleonic Wars that he is best remembered. As a side achievement he established a positive control of large parts of Europe that his army had conquered. His rule unfortunately became an autocratic one. Due to his many successes on the battle field, he still is considered to be one or the greatest military commanders of all time. His campaigns are still studied at Military Academies all over the World.

The paradox is that he was not a French man by birth. He was born in Corsica on 15 August in 1769, and his military training was as an artillery officer in the French Army.

The events that led to his eventual leadership of the French armies were his successful campaigns against the First and Second Coalition that were arrayed against him.

It was in 1799 that he took over the role as the leader of France by force, and installed himself as First Consul. Later he declared himself Emperor of France. In the first ten years of the 19th century his armies were involved in a series of conflicts with other European Countries.

Despite his successes on the battlefield, against an array of opponents, his campaign against Russia proved his undoing. His army was caught in one of the terrible winters that occur routinely in that part of the world. An enormous number of his soldiers died in a painful retreat through hundreds of miles of ice and snow.

It was in 1813 that his forces were defeated by the Sixth Coalition at the battle of Leipzig. It was in the following year, after this defeat, that the Coalition invaded France and forced him to escape to the island of Elba. Less than a year later he escaped from the island and attempted to return to power. However, he was defeated in the battle of Waterloo by the British in June of 1815. The last six years of his life were spent in confinement on the British Island of Saint Helena, which is located in the Mediterranean.

The significant thing, pertaining to the subject of this book, is an Order he issued to his officers while he was still in power. This Order must have been issued early in the 19th Century. The nature of the Order was, "To find a way of communicating in total darkness, without using a light of any kind."

Strangely, this Order which was only intended to help his armies win battles on the Battlefield, became the catalyst that led to the creation of the Braille Code.

Captain Charles Barbier de la serre

This Officer, apparently, was the only one who responded and offered a proposed method of communicating in total darkness.

He named the method he proposed "Ecriture Noctune" which is translated as "Night Writing."

His proposal was related to the Polybius Square. This square incorporates a two digit code where each number represents a letter in the French Alphabet. This Square consisted of a 6 by 6 square. The squares incorporate letters and diagraphs and trigraphs.

The afore mentioned digraph or trigraph had two columns of dots. The first column had 1 to 6 dots which identified the row and another 1 to 6 dots that identified the column. As an example, the letter "t" would be represented by the numbers 4-2 or row 4 column 2.

The system gets rather bulky because the term "ieu", which is a letter in the French Alphabet, is identified by the numbers 6-6 or row 6 and column 6. Trying to use a method in the dark like this one would undoubtedly be a challenge.

Anyway, the French Army rejected his Method because it was too complicated. But, according to the records, Captain Barbier was not a man to give up easily. It seems he had almost fallen in love with his own creativity; which turned out to be a blessing, because his persistence finally brought success.

The critical thing was that he presented his Method to the School for the Blind. A young boy, by the name of Louis Braille, was in attendance at that school when he was 9 years old and attended the presentation. It was a tangled web of circumstances that became obstacles to the Captains persistent efforts to get his Method accepted. However, he met resistance after resistance by influential individuals that he contacted.

There seems to be a built in resistance by most

people to accept something new and foreign to what they have encountered all of their life.

For example, in the year 1819 on the 28th day of June a meeting of the Academy of Sciences was held in Paris. One of the main subjects brought before the members was to consider a letter from the Captain to the Board.

The Board was informed that "an invention of a new machine which engraves a writing secret combinations without its being necessary to see the equipment." If his intent was to confuse these over educated stuff shirts, he succeeded.

They didn't have the faintest idea what he was proposing, even after he tried to explain it. So, they collectively did the red blooded thing and assigned a Committee to study the Proposal. This is usually an iron clad way to make a problem go away. The Committee ordinarily studies the idea to death and nothing of any importance comes of it.

The appointees were a Messrs. Prony and a Messrs. Lacepede. These two individuals produced a voluminous Report that would bore any rational person to death. The only sentence in the Report that made any sense was the statement of "This process makes communication between the deaf and blind possible". To say the least, the statement itself is terribly misleading. What should have been said was that "it provided the Blind with a method of reading the written word by using the sense of touch only".

The Captain's experience in Artillery, in Louis XVIII's Army, had caused him to notice how difficult it was to transmit orders in nighttime maneuvers. Transmitting orders verbally sometimes changed with each person passing on the order. The Captain came to the conclusion that the answer to the problem was to be able to transmit orders in some manner like an order in writing.

He named his second attempt "Sonography". The words were written phonetically. It required a great many dots and was long and difficult to use.

Eventually, perhaps in desperation, the Captain visited the School for the blind in Paris. Perhaps in his determination to get someone to listen to him and give their blessing, the place to go was a place that taught the blind.

He had the naïve notion that Mr. Guillie

would welcome his proposal. He guessed wrong again. R. Guillie pulled the old Stall Technique, which is a second cousin to the Committee Method. His response was that the method would have to have lengthy testing by the blind students first.

What it really meant was he was giving Captain Barbier the Old Kiss Off Treatment hoping he would just go away. It seems that once Mr. Guillie made up his mind, he wasn't to be confused by further facts of any kind.

He left the School a bit disappointed, but he was a very stubborn man.

Just at that time, an event occurred that helped the Captain pursue his goal. Mr. Guillie had been caught with his hand in the cookie jar, in a manner of speaking. He was caught carrying on a bit of hanky panky with one of the women on the Staff and was summarily discharged.

This fortunate incident, at least from Captain Barbier's perspective, led to the replacement of Messrs. Guillee by a Messrs.Pignier.

For the first time, the Captain had found someone whose mind was not closed like a bear trap. However, initially even Messrs. Pignier also had his doubts, because of the complexity of the Captains Sonography Method.

The new Director of the School called all thirty of the students together and explained to them the history of the Captain's Invention of Sonography. Louis Braille was one of the students in that group. The Captain had left a few embossed pages with the Director, who passed them around to each of the students.

There really wasn't anything of lasting importance except for one thing, and that was the Staff and the students at the School became interested in this New Method.

Louis Braille, after attending the presentation, had been trying, on his own time, to find a way to help other people like himself, who were blind, to be able to read easily.

When he passed his fingers over the dots, he suddenly realized this was what he had been searching for.

The students became excited and questioned the Director and tried to read the words that the Captain had left. The consensus by the students was that the New System should be adopted.

The Captain was informed by the Director, that his Sonography would be used by the Institution as an "Auxiliary teaching method."

Louis Braille had a friend who also was a blind student at the school. The two practiced every spare moment they had between their studies. They tried sending and reading messages to each other.

The Embossed Writing the Captain had left had been written by using a clever device, which consisted of a two edged board equipped with a sliding rule. The ruler was pierced with small windows, which permitted a blind person to trace dots. This was done with precision by using a stylus. The stylus embossed the heavy paper which had been placed between the ruler and the board.

Over a period of time, Louis began to learn more about the Captain's way of writing in code in the dark. He learned that the code was intended to be used to deliver messages at night from the officers to the soldiers. The messages could not be written on paper, because the soldier would have to strike a match to read it.

The light from the match would give the

enemy a target at which to shoot. The alphabet code was made up of small dots and dashes. These symbols were raised up off the paper, so that soldiers could read them by running their fingers over them. Once the soldiers understood the code, they would be able to translate it into words.

Once Louis had obtained copies of the Captains Code he found out it was much easier to read than the bulky books with the large raised letters.

But the Army code was still slow and cumbersome. The dashes took up a lot of space on a page. Each page could only hold one or two sentences. He felt that he could improve this alphabet in some way.

On his next vacation at home, he spent all his spare time working on finding a way to make this improvement. When he arrived home for school vacation, he was greeted warmly by his parents.

It was reported that he would find a grassy knoll and sit down and begin poking holes in a piece of leather. He was searching for just the right way to accomplish what he had in mind.

Passer-bys would shake there heads, meanwhile wondering what he was trying to do.

Also, his mother and father always encouraged him in his music and other school projects. He sat down to think about how he could improve the system of dots and dashes. He liked the idea of the raised dots, but came to the conclusion that the dashes could be dispensed with.

One day while in his father's leather shop, he picked up one of his father's awls. The idea came to him in a flash. The very tool which had caused him to go blind could be used to make a raised dot alphabet that would enable him to read.

The next few days he spent working on an alphabet made up entirely of six dots on one of six squares. The position of the different dots would represent the different letters of the alphabet.

Louis used the awl to punch out a sentence. He read it quickly from left to right, and came to believe that at last he was near his goal.

Back at the school, shortly after the Captain had presented his Sonography Program, he and a friend began practicing with it. During any leisure time, Louis and his friend Gauthier would practice writing sentences to each other and try to read them back. They used the writing device the Captain had left at the school.

As Louis and his friend became increasingly familiar with the Captain's Method, he began to find flaws in the System.

After much practicing with the Board, Louis began to perceive some short comings in Sonography. It resembled the current Shorthand taught in the past in business colleges. It was not built around conventional rules of spelling. Instead the dots represented sounds only.

There was no provision for punctuation and numbers etc. The biggest objection was its complexity and the attendant difficulty in reading Sonography.

By his persistence, and his innate skill in analyzing and making constructive changes and modifications, Louis improved the Captain's Sonography System.

Louis then proceeded to inform the Director, Messesr. Pignier. The Director in turn contacted the Captain and informed him that a student recommended certain changes in his invention.

The Captain was impressed and hurried to the school to interview this student. When he was introduced to Louis, to his astonishment the student was an eleven year old boy who was very thin and pale and had blond hair. In addition, Louis was completely blind.

Then he was even more astonished, when this mere boy began politely to call his attention to the flaws (in his opinion) in the System. Louis pointed out the obvious drawbacks of the Captains Invention; at least they appeared to be drawbacks to him. Also he had the temerity of suggesting several major changes, to rub a little salt in the wound. At least the Captain considered it temerity for such a young boy, still wet behind the ears, to be suggesting that he knew more than the Captain. Heaven forbid!

Apparently, the self assurance and confidence with which Louis handled him self tended to set the Captain aback. What upset him the most was that he had to admit, at least to himself, that this young pipsqueak of a boy was one hundred percent right. To a man like the Captain, who had attained the age of 55 years, with many years of commanding large groups of men in battle, this was a somewhat painful experience. He then proceeded to defend his Invention in a very dominant forceful manner. This intimidated Louis so much that he took the wise course and quietly withdrew from the confrontation.

But, even though, this somewhat finished the Captain's involvement in the further development of the Raised Dot System; Louis was just beginning to make progress in his effort to make reading for the blind much easier.

However, at this point, it is proper to honor the Good Captain. It was because of his dedication to what he considered a worthwhile cause and his persistence in the face of continued resistance that he finally succeeded. Those who experience sight impairment should always be grateful for his invaluable contributions. It is undoubtedly true that initially his helping the Blind was not his primary purpose. Being a military person, he was focused on winning on the battlefield. But, it is just possible, after interviewing the students at the School for the Blind his focus changed. Maybe he developed a compassion for the young blind students who had to carry such a heavy cross at such an early age or at any age for that matter.

So a Salute to Captain Charles Barbier de la serre!

Louis's Struggle to Perfect his Braille Code

During this overall creative period there had been nights when Louis got very little sleep, which adversely affected his health.

Almost all night long he would mentally wrestle with the problem. He tried strictly on his own to perfect a system, that at the time he had only a faint idea of what it would be like when it was finished.

Finally, after several school years had come and gone, at the end of one summers vacation, he had improved his Proposed System to the point that it was ready to be unveiled. He first confided to his friend Gauthier. Gauthier then announced it to the rest of the students and also to Mr. Pignier.

When Mr. Pignier heard about Louis's New System he had him summoned to his office. As Louis sat there comfortably in a large arm-chair opposite the Director, he began his demonstration. Mr. Pignier was amazed by its simplicity and rapidity of execution. He embraced the boy and provided him with fatherly encouragement. This acceptance by the Director provided him with added resolve.

Meanwhile, the other students adopted the new Braille Code with enthusiasm. The Director had Barbier's Sliding Rule converted.

The students could now take notes in class; do their spelling, write composition letters and copy items from books. They also, for the first time, could correspond with each other.

In spite of his success, Louis did not neglect his studies and always ranked near the top of his class. Among the things he accomplished were, that at fourteen years of age, he was foreman of a workshop that made slippers.

When he was only seventeen years old, while he was only a student, he began to teach algebra, grammar and geography. He studied the Organ at the College de France and gave piano lessons to other students.

In 1827 his new Braille made it possible to transcribe parts of the Grammar of Grammars.

In 1828 he branched out into the field of music notation. He wrote notes in seven different octaves by assigning a symbol that preceded each octave.

In 1829 he presented his first edition of the "Method of Writing Words, Music and Plain Songs" by means of dots, for use by the blind and arranged for them.

It was in the Preface of Louis' book that he paid tribute to all of the contributions made by Captain Charles Barbier.

Louis Braille was a very humble man, who shunned the spotlight and his life serves as an example, and an inspiration, in the way each of us should strive to live ours.

The Contributions by Mr. Pignier

It would not be seemly to close out this section of the book without acknowledging the many contributions made by Mr. Pignier. He was, without a doubt, a kind, compassionate man, who recognized a God given talent in a frail little boy and did everything in his power to assist him in realizing his dream.

Such Men Like Mr. Pignier Have Helped Change The World in Meaningful Ways!

The Louis Braille System

For those not familiar with this Code, it is simply a system of reading text represented by a number of raised dots in one of six squares. It allows individuals, who have visual impairment of different degrees, to read using the sense of touch. These individuals may be completely or partially blind. Others not only have a visual impairment, but also may have a serious hearing impairment.

It is true that blind persons who were introduced to the system adopted it immediately. However, educators of blind students did not officially adopt the System until thirty years later in 1854.

The suggested reluctance for teachers of the blind to accept it was their fear it would cause them to lose their jobs. Also, rooted in this resistance was the built in bias against anything new and different.

The Braille System itself consists of six squares. These squares are arranged in a grid which is two squares wide and three squares high. With this simple arrangement there are 63 combinations of raised dots. Also, in addition, over time, 189 contractions have been developed and used.

Such a simple basic system has had an incredibly complex system superimposed on it.

There are several grades of Braille. Number one grade is Louis Braille's basic system. Grade two was developed in England, and in 1932 it was adopted as the Braille of choice for all English speaking nations.

The biggest drawbacks for Braille are that it is bulky and it is necessary to print on thick paper or plastic sheets. A Braille press, writer, computer printer or a manual slate and a stylus is needed to write Braille.

As stated earlier, the raised dots are sensed by the individuals using finger tips. Both hands are required, one hand must be used to do the actual reading, and the other hand is used in helping the reader keep his place. The average reading speed by those skilled in this sort of thing is about 104 words per minute. Some exceptionally skilled readers of Braille, who specialize in reading with both hands, have been able to read at 200 words per minute.

According to the information available, Braille does not serve all persons with sight and/or sound impairment. Some have enough vision to still read with instruments that greatly enlarge the words. Others do not have enough sensitivity in their finger tips that is due to a number of health reasons or otherwise. Also, many individuals rely on books that have been recorded on Audio CD's etc. However, in the parts of the world where money is scarce Braille still thrives due to necessity.

Interestingly enough there is a paperless Braille. This Information Systems is stored on disks. This method of Versabraille requires several pieces of equipment. The individual reads a line and the device then loads the next line or sentence.

The First Braille Writer

This device, as the name implies, is used to write Braille. It resembles a typewriter and in earlier times was manual instead of electric. It had been proven to be more efficient than the manual slate and stylus method.

The first Brailler was the Hall Braillewriter which was invented by Frank H. Hall in 1892. At the time he was Superintendent of the Illinois School for the Blind.

Braille writers of that era had six keys and a space bar. The user doing the writing in Braille had to press the proper levers to emboss the letter which was desired at the moment.

It is stated that Braille writers vary in size. Usually they were fifteen inches by five inches by five inches and weighed about ten pounds. Current Braille writers at the time this information was issued included the Perkins Brailler, the Lavender Braillewriter and the Hall Braillewriter.

On the following pages is a Review of
The Four Events that led to the creation of the Braille Code:

Event No. 1
The Storming of the Bastille in Paris

Event No. 2
Louis XVI Ruled France
As King from 1774-1792

King Louis XVI was executed by being guillotined on January 21, 1793. He had tried to escape from France in June of 1791 and was captured. The French Monarchy then was abolished and a Republic was proclaimed.

Below is a Picture of his Execution...

Journeé du 21 Janvier 1793.
la mort de Louis Capet sur la Place de la Revolution
Presentée a la Convention Nationale
le 21 Germinal par H. chuain

Note:

In the left center of the photograph the Executioner is holding up the Former Kings severed head for the benefit of the Mob.

His wife, Marie Antoinette, was executed on October 16, 1793. The Paris Mob didn't have mercy on anyone. It is estimated that up to as many as 40,000 individuals were executed with the guillotine.

Event No. 3

General Bonaparte is shown here surrounded by members of the Council of Five Hundred just prior to taking over as Emperor of France on November 9, 1799. During the latter part of his reign he issued an order to all his Officers to find a way of conveying orders at night in total darkness.

Event No. 4
Captain Charles Barbier de la serre

De Serre.

Captain Barbier was the only Officer in Napoleon's Army who complied with the Order, at least according to the Records.

Charles Barbier's Night Writing Grid

	1	2	3	4	5	6
1	a	i	o	u	e'	e'
2	an	in	on	un	eu	ou
3	b	d	g	j	v	z
4	p	t	q	ch	f	s
5	l	m	n	r	gn	ll
6	oi	oin	ian	ien	ion	ieu

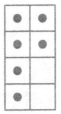

Note: Fig #2 represents the letter "t" in Fig. #1.

The 4 dots on the left represents counting down 4 rows in column #1 and the two dots in the right column represents counting along row 2 two squares.

Event No. 5
A Picture of Louis Braille

He simplified Captain Barbier's
Night Writing System
to the following format:

Louis Braille's Original Code

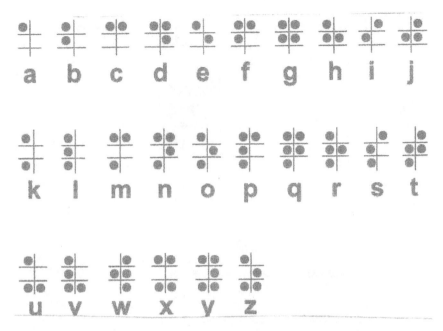

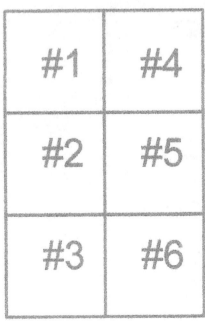

Louis Braille's Original Code

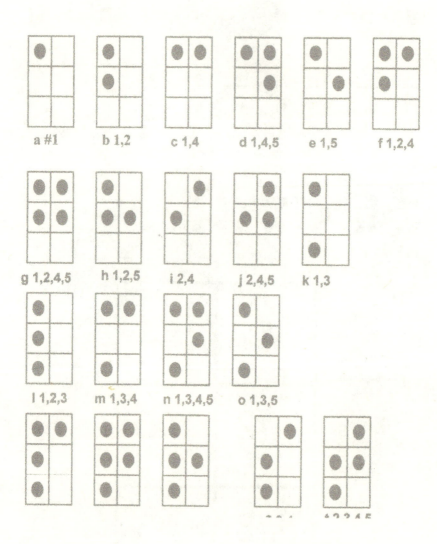

Louis Braille's Code (cont'd)

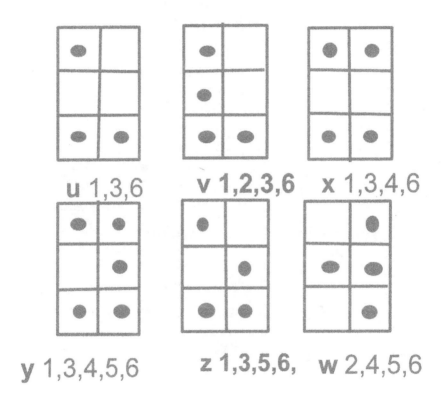

u 1,3,6   v **1,2,3,6**   x 1,3,4,6

y 1,3,4,5,6   z **1,3,5,6,**   w 2,4,5,6

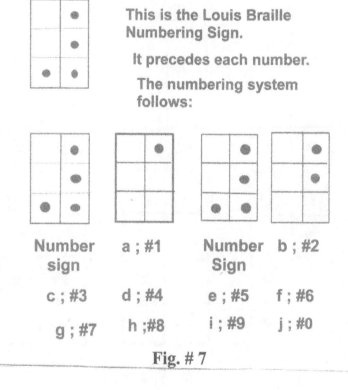

This is the Louis Braille Numbering Sign.

It precedes each number.

The numbering system follows:

Number sign	a ; #1	Number Sign	b ; #2
c ; #3	d ; #4	e ; #5	f ; #6
g ; #7	h ;#8	i ; #9	j ; #0

Fig. # 7

Note:
There is a number sign after each number.

Note:
The selection of dots and their arrangement is not related one with another. There is a lack of correlation. Each grid pattern for each letter must be learned separately. Therefore, there are 26 different patterns to be learned. To write Braille all letter dot patterns must be learned in reverse making it necessary to learn 52 patterns.
Braille must be learned in reverse, because Braille is written from the underside of the page. If it was 'written' in the correct order it would be in reverse on the top of the page.

Robert Richey's Revised Braille Grid Numbering System

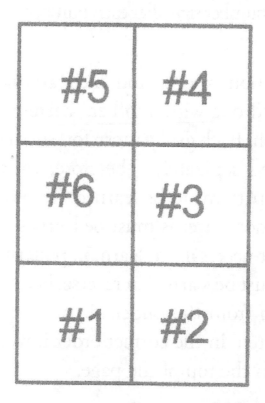

Note: the Order of the appearance of the 6 numbers is in a counter clock wise direction.

Robert Richey's Revised Braille

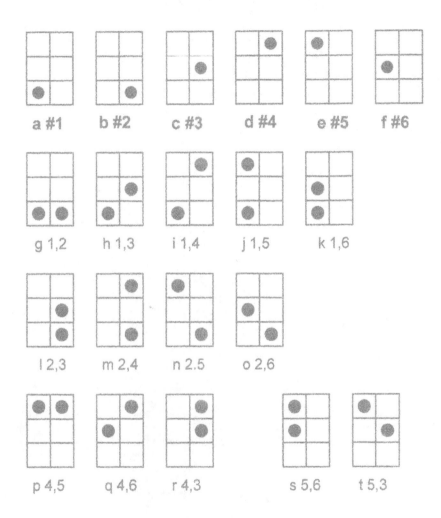

Note:

The same counter clock wise rule still applies.

Robert Richey's Revised Braille (Page 2 cont'd)

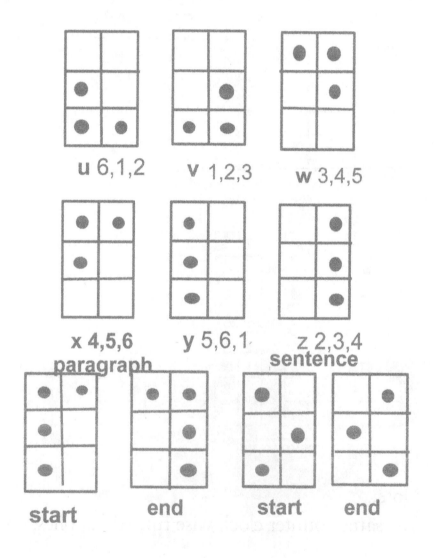

u 6,1,2   v 1,2,3   w 3,4,5

x 4,5,6   y 5,6,1   z 2,3,4
paragraph   sentence

start   end   start   end

A Revised Braille Numbering System

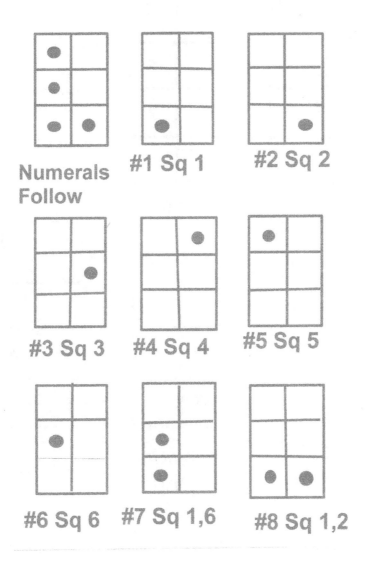

Numerals cont'd

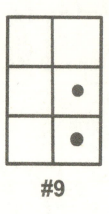

#9

#0

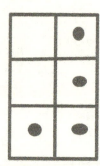

end of numerals

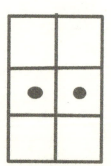

Indicates a space

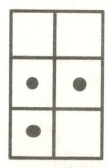

Indicates a period

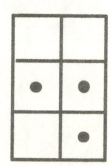

Indicates a colon

Note:

The dots shown in the above figures represent tips of the spindles in the various blocks in the Robert Richey revised Braille Reader. The blocks and the spindles will be discussed later in the book. The Actuator(s) will also be discussed later in the book. An Actuator causes the individual spindle to rise to the fully upright position and to return to the fully retracted position,

Note:

The simplicity of the Proposed Revised Braille Code. For example: If there is the tip of one Spindle protruding out of the face of a Block and there is no second Tip then the letter is "a" thru "f". The letters occur in a counter clockwise direction like the Revised Grid numbering system.

Instance #2:

If there are two tips protruding and one tip is always in Square #1 then the letters are "g" through "k".

Instance #3:

If there are two tips protruding and one of the

tips is always in Square #2 then the letters are "l" through "o".

Instance #4:

If there are two tips protruding and one of the tips is always in Square #4 the letters are "p" through "r".

Instance #5:

If there are two tips protruding and one of the tips is always in Square #5 the letters are "s" through "t".

Instance #6:

If there are always three tips protruding and one of the tips is the center tip of the three and is in Square #1 it is letter "u"; If one of the tips is the center of the 3 tips and is in Square #2 it is the letter "v"; If one of the tips protruding is the center tip of the 3 and is in Square 4 it is letter "w"; If one of the tips protruding is the center of the 3 and is in Square #5 it is letter "x"; If three tips are protruding out of the individual block and all of the tips are in squares 1, 5 and 6 it is the letter "y"; If three tips are protruding out of the individual block and all of the tips are in squares 2, 3 and 4 it is the letter "z".

Robert Richey's Dynamic Braille Reading System for the Use of the Individual with Visual Sight Impairment

Robert Richey's System

Consists of the following:

1. A Simplified Micro Computer
   a. This device is required to activate electrical switches Off or On in response to the Installed Computer Program.
2. A CD or Flash Memory USB Port
3. A Direct Current
   a. A source of electricity that can be from a DC Generator or a Rechargeable/Portable Battery Pack.
4. A Series of Blocks
5. A Special Program on a CD for instructions to the Computer to activate the various Electrical Switches in the Overall Operation of the System
6. A Set of six (6) Spindles for each Block
7. A Pair of On/Off electrical Switches that are Computer actuated for each of the six Spindles in each Block
8. A Set of Mating Male and Female plug-in Boards per Spindle
9. A pair of Electrical One Way Current

Flow Devices for each Spindle Assembly wiring.

10.   A set of 6 soft rubber washers to be installed with each of the 6 Spindles in each Block.

11.   An Actuation Device for raising and lowering each Spindle on Computer Command

12.   A Separate Command Panel provided for the use of the Operator (i.e. the Blind Person).

Clock Wise is in the direction of 12 to 3 to 6 to 9 back to 12

Clock

12

9

3

6

Counter Clock Wise is from 12 to 9 to 6 to 3 and back to 12.

Robert Richey's Dynamic Braille Reader Cont'd

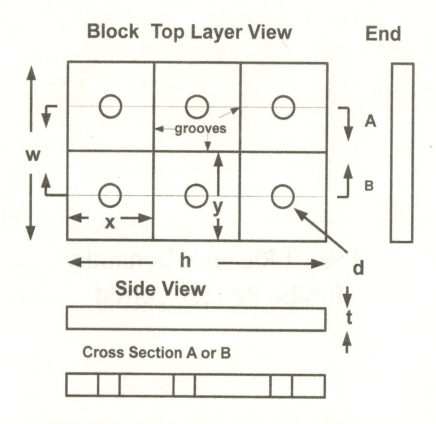

Block Top Layer View   **End**

grooves

w

x

A

B

y

h

d

Side View

t

Cross Section A or B

Indicates Cross-Sectional Views thru the circle centers

$x = y$
$d = y/4$
$t = y/2$

$w = 2y$
$h = 3x$

Note:

The three layers are cut through each Block along the center line of the three holes on each side. This is done to facilitate the insertion of the Spindle Assemblies in the sockets for the 6 squares in each and every Block. The Blocks can be made out of extruded plastic, wood or other materials.

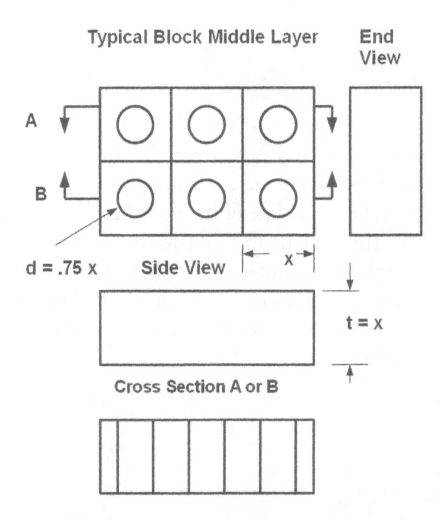

Typical Block Middle Layer   End View

A

B

d = .75 x   Side View |← x →|

t = x

Cross Section A or B

A Typical Block

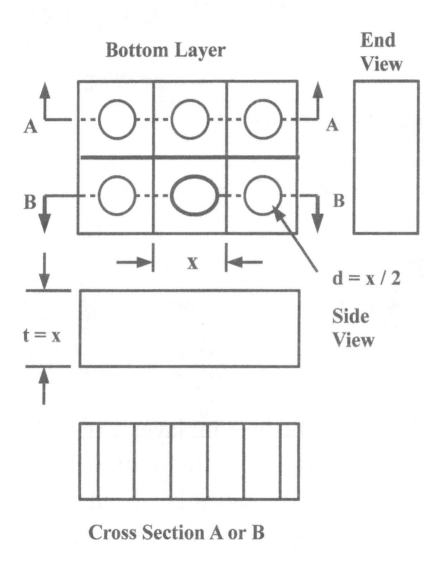

Bottom Layer

End View

A   A

B   B

x

$d = x / 2$

$t = x$

Side View

Cross Section A or B

Top View of the Middle Layer
of a Model Shown Without Spindles

Shown is the bottom layer under the
middle layer with the smaller holes
displayed. The Block has been cut in
two along the 3 holes centerline.

Top View of a Middle Layer in Place Shown With 3 Spindles in Place

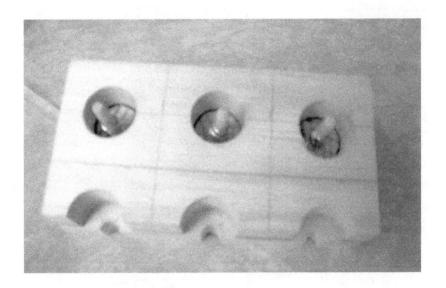

Note:

The Spindles shown are not the production items, but are shown to convey the design of the individual blocks. A cut-away side view is shown with three Spindles in place.

Shown Below is a Typical Block

Note:

Three layers of a Block are shown, but the thickness of the three layers differs from the actual production item. In this photo the tips of all six spindles are shown in the full upright position.

This Block was constructed by a friend, Bill Strandberg.

Spindle Cross Sectional View

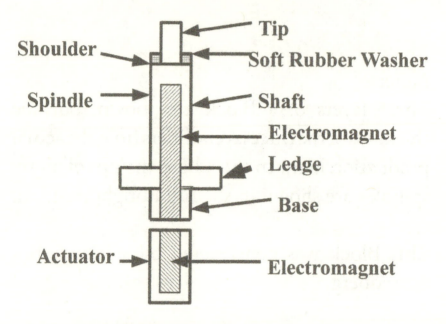

**Note: Electromagnets are encased
In plastic**

A Typical Spindle in a typical Block Shown in the down; not actuated position

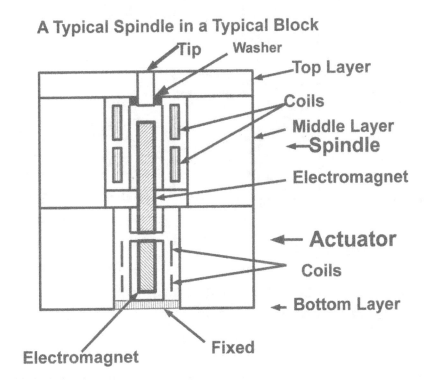

A Typical Spindle in a Typical Block

Tip   Washer
Top Layer
Coils
Middle Layer
Spindle
Electromagnet
Actuator
Coils
Bottom Layer
Electromagnet   Fixed

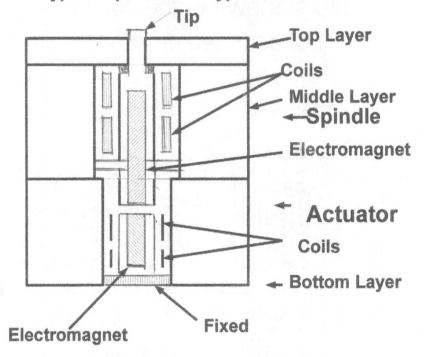

A Typical Spindle in a Typical Block

In the spindle upright position
With the tip exposed

Fig # 21

The Actuators

Each Spindle has an Actuator. This device operates on magnetic principles. The Actuator causes the individual Spindle to rise to its full upright position on Computer Command and to return to the down position when a reverse force is applied. This reverse force is assisted by the compressive force of a soft rubber washer. Each Spindle is equipped with a soft rubber washer.

The Principle of Magnets

Many substances have some degree of magnetism, but it is so weak that the attraction and repulsion features cannot be sensed.

The materials that demonstrate the strongest magnetism are iron, nickel, cobalt and alloys of rare earth metals. If soft iron is exposed to a certain treatment, it converts it into a permanent magnet. This type magnet is called a ferrimagnet.

Other types' of magnets are called ferromagnets. These magnets are temporarily magnetized. Their magnetism only exists when the metal is in a magnetic field. Annealed iron is the most common metal used for electromagnets.

The atoms in iron are magnetic due to their atomic structure and demonstrate a north and south pole characteristic. If these atoms exist in disarray the metal displays very little magnetism. However, if many of the atoms are aligned in the north /south direction, they reinforce each other and their repelling or attracting forces can be very strong.

If a piece of insulated copper wire is made into a coil, and a direct current is caused to flow through the coil, it will become magnetized. Apparently, the flow of electrons through the coil causes this to happen.

The direction in which the wire is coiled determines which end of the coil is the North Pole or the South Pole.

If the wire is coiled in the counter clock wise direction, as viewed from the upper end, the North Pole will be at the top of the coil. If the wire is coiled in the clock wise direction, as viewed from the upper end, the North Pole will be at the bottom of the coil.

No one understands magnetism. They only know how it performs. Although, copper is not one of the stronger magnetic type metals, it is possible that the flow of electrons through the copper in the coil causes it to become magnetized. It is known that electrons orbit in rings in various materials

If, a piece of soft (annealed) iron (un-magnetized) is placed in a coil of insulated copper wire and a direct current of electricity is passed through the wire the iron will be become magnetized. When the current is turned off, the iron returns to its un-magnetized state.

The Rules of Magnetism are associated with the Right Hand Rule.

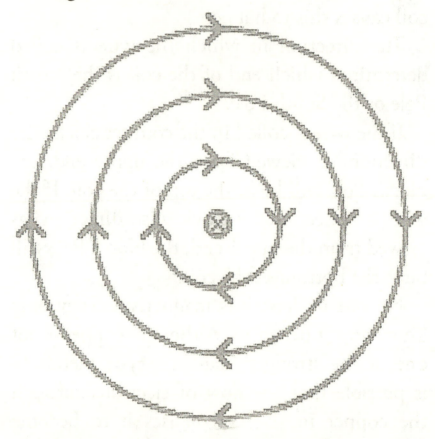

In the above figure, it is assumed that the circle in the center represents a cross section of a soft iron bar with direct current flowing into the paper. The outer circles with the arrow heads (clock wise direction), represent the direction the wire is wrapped. If the iron bar protrudes out of the paper, and an individual wraps the fingers of the right hand around this bar in the direction of the arrows, the thumb would be pointed into the paper. The thumb would be pointing at the other end of the bar and it would be the North Pole.

North

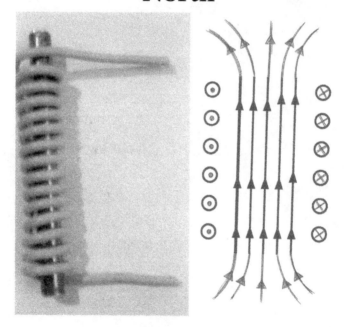

South

North Pole

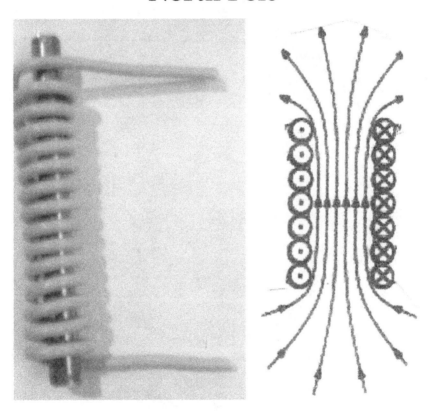

South Pole

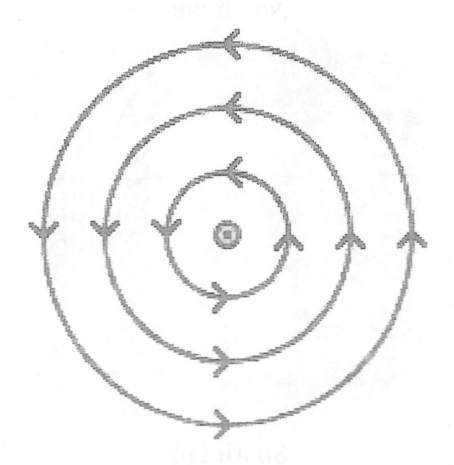

In the preceding figures, it is assumed that it represents a cross section of a coil of copper wire with direct current flowing into the paper on the left side of the coil. Following the Right Hand Rule the polarity would be as shown. The circles with the x's in the center represent dc current flowing into the paper. The circles having dots in the center represent dc current flowing out from the paper. It is like an arrow that has been bent into a half circular shape, where the x's are the feather of the arrow, and the dots are the tip of the arrow heads.

If on the other hand, the direct current direction of flow was reversed, the magnetic field would also be reversed. If again the fingers of the right hand were wrapped around the bar in the direction of the arrows, the near end of the wire would be the North Pole.

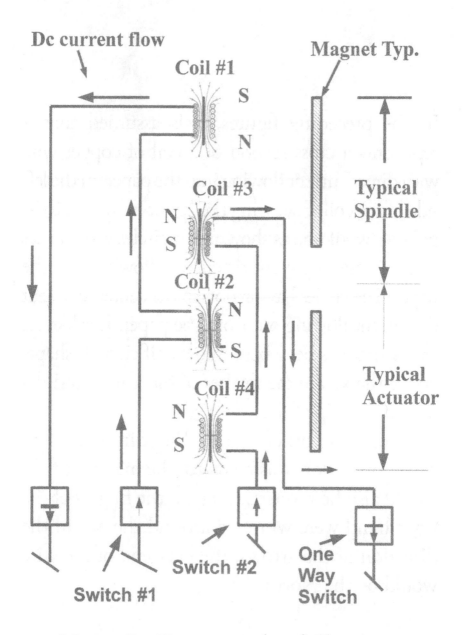

Note: In Fig. #26 the following applies:

Coils #1 & #2 are connected in series. Coil #1 is wrapped around the shaft of each Spindle. Coil #2 is wrapped around the Actuator. Switch #1 in each of six (6) Spindle Circuits is connected in series with the coils #1 and #2. A one way electrical flow device is connected in series with coils #1 and # 2 for each spindle/actuator. Refer to Fig. #29 on page 88.The North Poles repel each other and the Spindle is forced into the full upright position.

Coils #3 and #4 are connected in series. Coil #3 is wrapped around the shaft of each Spindle. Coil #4 is wrapped around the Actuator. Switch #2 in each of the six (6) Spindle Circuits is connected in series with coils #3 and #4. A one way electrical flow device is connected in series with coils #3 and #4. Refer to Fig. # 29 on page 88. The South Pole of coil #3 and the North Pole of coil #4 attract each other and force the Spindle to the fully retracted position.

The point being made here is that the polarity of the field can be reversed by reversing the direction of the flow of the direct current. Alternating current will not follow the Right Hand Rule, as it is changing the direction of current flow rapidly.

If the wire is wrapped around a piece of annealed iron, its polarity will be the same. The polarity of the iron is determined by the direction of flow of the direct current and the Right Hand Rule applies.

The Right Hand Rule applied is as follows: if the right hand is wrapped around the electromagnet with the fingers in the direction of the magnetic field as shown, the North Pole is in the direction that the thumb points.

South

North

North

South

If the two (2) North Poles are in proximity to each other they will repel each other.

Assuming the bar at the top is one of a number of Spindles, and the bar at the bottom is the Actuating Magnet, the following applies: if the Actuating Magnet is fixed, the repelling force between them will force the Upper magnet (Spindle) upward. This small movement will cause the tip of a particular Spindle to protrude out of its hole and the tip will be exposed.

In the Production Model the two coils are connected in series.

North

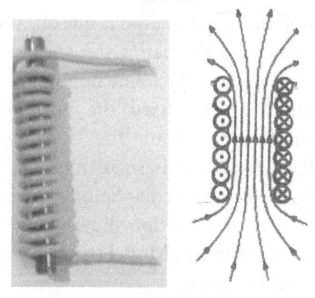

South

North

 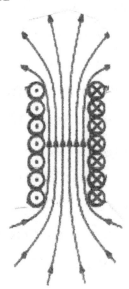

South

In Fig. #29A & 29B on the previous page the wire in both coils has been wrapped in a counter clock wise direction. This results in both bars (electromagnets) having the North Pole on the upper end.

If the two electromagnets are placed near each other as shown, the South Pole of the magnet at the top and the North Pole of the magnet at the bottom will attract each other.

If the electromagnet at the top represents a particular Spindle and: the electromagnet at the bottom represents the Actuator and the Actuator is fixed in place; the attractive force between them will cause the Spindle to move downward till it bottoms out.

In the Production Model the two coils are connected in series.

Revised Braille Grid

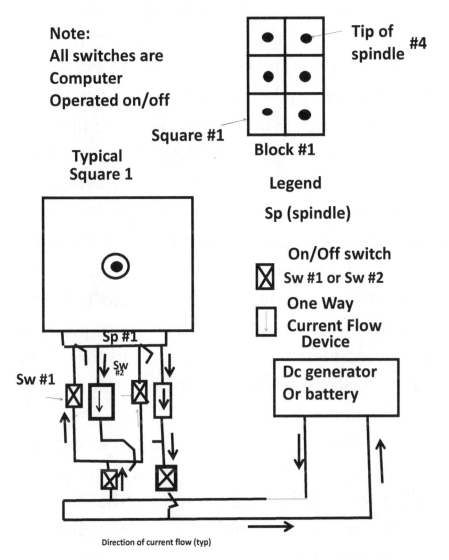

Note:
All switches are
Computer
Operated on/off

Tip of
spindle **#4**

Square #1

Typical
Square 1

Block #1

Legend

Sp (spindle)

On/Off switch
Sw #1 or Sw #2

One Way
Current Flow
Device

Sp #1

Sw #2

Sw #1

Dc generator
Or battery

Direction of current flow (typ)

Note: The switches are placed in the open or closed position on Computer command

95

If for example the wire in Fig. # 28 A & 28 B is continuous and is wound around both electromagnets, the dc current flows through both of them. The switch in line(Switch # 1) with this pair of coils as shown in Fig, # 30 will cause the Spindle in question to move upward.

If the wire in Fig. # 28A & # 28 B is continuous and is wound around both electromagnets the dc current through one is through both. The other switch in line (Switch # 2) will cause the particular Spindle to move downward.

Therefore, if both pairs of wire coils are wound around either of the two pairs of electromagnets then Switch # 1 and Switch #2 can reverse the polarity of the upper and lower electromagnets.

The closing of Switch #1, on Computer command, will result in the particular Spindle rising to its full upright position (the shoulder on the individual Spindle Shaft limits how far it can move upward.)

If Switch #1 is placed in the off position, on Computer command, and Switch #2 is placed in the on position the Spindle will be lowered to its original bottom out position. The soft rubber washers help keep each Spindle in the down position when the #1 switch is in the off position.

Each Spindle has its own pair of dc electric circuits and is controlled separately by a pair of on/off switches. Each one can be activated independently.

In addition, the wiring in the return flow in each dc circuit has a one way electrical device that prevents any back flow of electricity.

In the Production Model all four coils are wound around only two soft iron bars.

Revised Braille Dynamic Reader

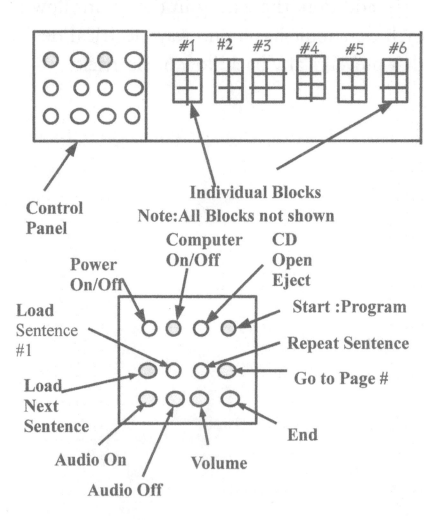

Control Panel

Individual Blocks
Note: All Blocks not shown

Power On/Off

Computer On/Off

CD Open Eject

Load Sentence #1

Start :Program

Load Next Sentence

Repeat Sentence

Go to Page #

Audio On

Audio Off

Volume

End

Programming

A Program must be written to be to be used in conjunction with the Braille Reader. This Program will convert the key strokes from the Computer Keyboard used in writing the Program. This conversion will provide the Computer with the capability of causing the proper Spindles to change to the full upright position in a particular block .This arrangement of Spindles will allow the blind person to read which key was struck.

To use the Reader the Blind Person would turn the Device on and pause while the Computer Booted up. A CD would be inserted in the drive for the particular book to be read in Braille and loaded.

The Audio Feature of the Control Panel (Ref. Fig. #31)could enable the User to be informed concerning various information, such as the Title of the Book, the name of the Author, the number of pages in the book and other related information.

With this advance information the Reader could then progress to loading the book one sentence at a time.

It is assume that there are twenty (20) individual blocks in a Rack with a small space between blocks. The blocks will be numbered from 1 to 20 from left to right.

For an Example a typical brief sentence will be demonstrated. The sentence reads as follows, "The cat ate the rat."

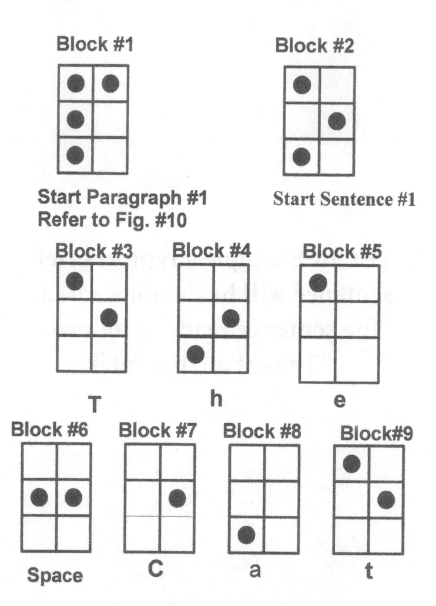

Block #1

**Start Paragraph #1
Refer to Fig. #10**

Block #2

Start Sentence #1

Block #3

T

Block #4

h

Block #5

e

Block #6

Space

Block #7

C

Block #8

a

Block#9

t

Sentence #1 continued

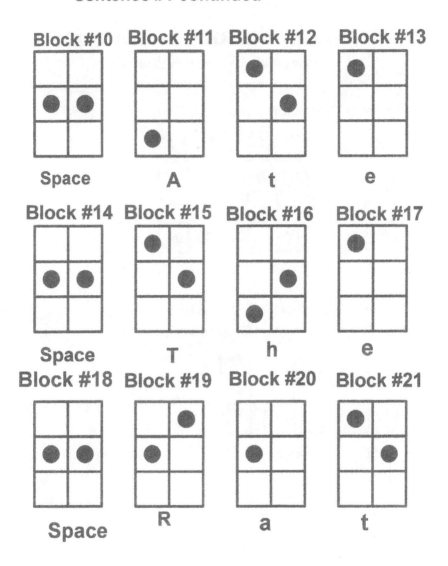

Block #10	Block #11	Block #12	Block #13
Space	A	t	e

Block #14	Block #15	Block #16	Block #17
Space	T	h	e

Block #18	Block #19	Block #20	Block #21
Space	R	a	t

Braille in Various Languages
French and Spanish in Braille

Quote "Viva La France"

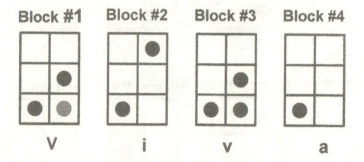

Quote in Spanish "Hasta La Vista"

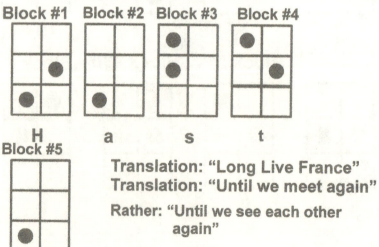

Translation: "Long Live France"
Translation: "Until we meet again"

Rather: "Until we see each other
            again"

Robert Richey's Revised Braille Grid Numbering System in Reverse

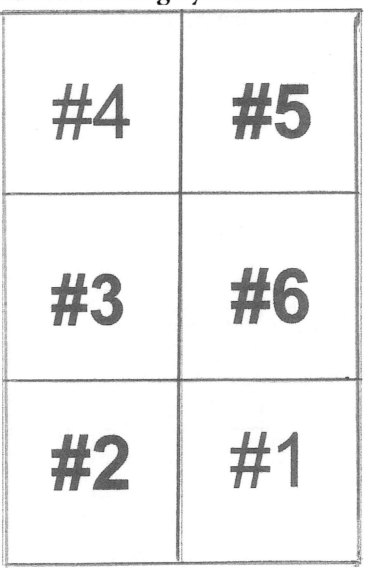

Robert Richey's Revised Reversed Braille Page 1

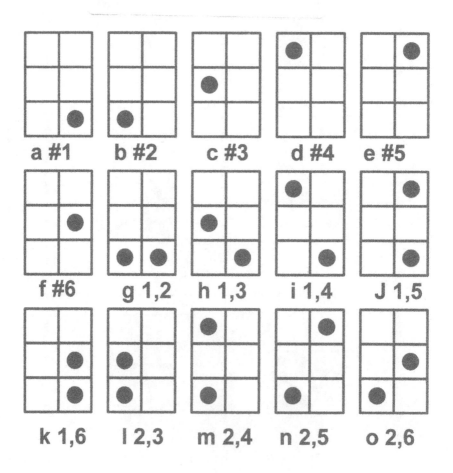

a #1   b #2   c #3   d #4   e #5

f #6   g 1,2   h 1,3   i 1,4   J 1,5

k 1,6   l 2,3   m 2,4   n 2,5   o 2,6

Robert Richey's Revised Reversed Braille Page 2

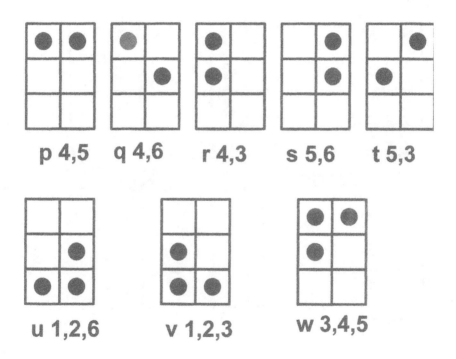

p 4,5   q 4,6   r 4,3   s 5,6   t 5,3

u 1,2,6   v 1,2,3   w 3,4,5

Robert Richey's Revised Reversed Braille Page 3

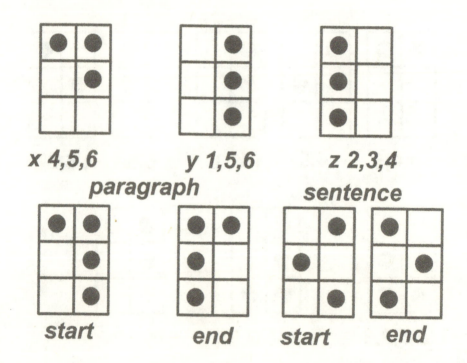

x 4,5,6   y 1,5,6   z 2,3,4

paragraph   sentence

start   end   start   end

A Reversed Braille Numbering System

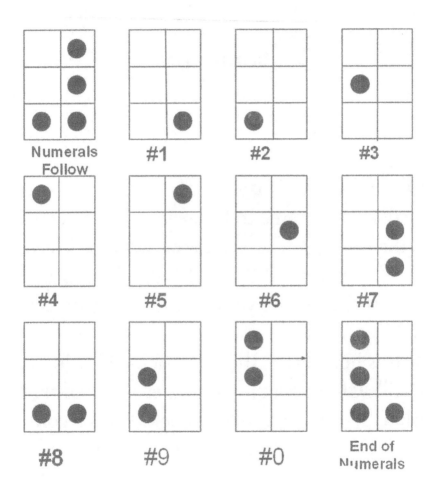

Summary

On the previous pages is the story of how the Braille Code came to be created. Also, detailed is the Robert Richey's Revised Braille Code and the Computerized Braille Reader. Finally is the Robert Richey's Reverse Braille Code for use in writing Braille.

It is hoped that this approach will bring the Braille Code into the Computer Age, and that a Blind person can read any book that is recorded on a CD instead of on so many books in the Current Braille.

Note; Any Reader of this book who wishes to discuss the contents, as related to Braille, with the Author, may do so at the Email Address:

rri6254288@sbcglobal.net